BOOM-BOOM-BAY!

by Mary Blocksma

Illustrated by Nancy Lane

HAMPTON-BROWN

Listen to the rainy day.
What does the thunder say?

The thunder goes,
"Boom-boom! Boom-boom!
Boom-boom-bay!"

Listen to the rainy day.
What does the rain say?
"Pit-a-pat! Pit-a-pat!"

And the thunder goes,
BOOM-BOOM-BAY!

Listen to the rainy day.
What does my umbrella say?
"Pop-pop! Pop-pop!"

And the thunder goes,

BOOM-BOOM-BAY!

Listen to the rainy day.
What does the hail say?
"Tack-a-tack! Tack-a-tack!"

And the thunder goes,

BOOM BOOM BAY!

Listen to the rainy day.
What does the pail say?
"Tink-tink! Tink-tink!"

And the thunder goes,

BOOM BOOM BAY!

Listen to the rainy day.
What does the water say?
"Whoosh! Whoosh!"

And the thunder goes,

BOOM
BOOM BAY!

Listen to the rainy day.
What does the day say?

"Pit-a-pat! Pit-a-pat!"
"Pop-pop! Pop-pop!"
"Tack-a-tack! Tack-a-tack!"
"Tink-tink! Tink-tink!"
"Whoosh! Whoosh!"